Pictures by **HILDEGARD WOODWARD**

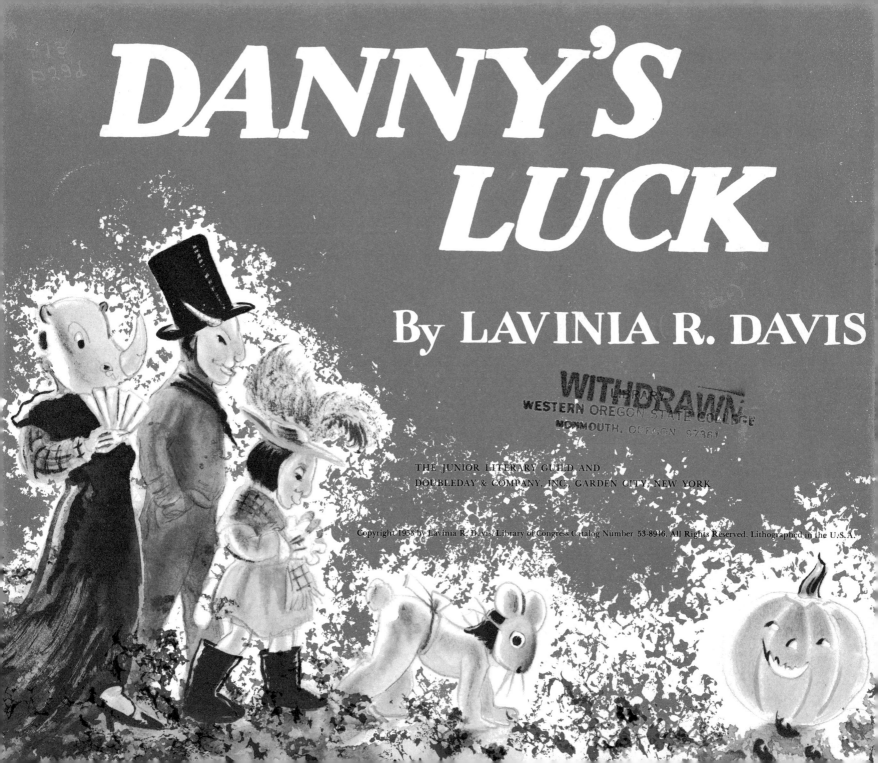

DANNY'S LUCK

By LAVINIA R. DAVIS

THE JUNIOR LITERARY GUILD AND
DOUBLEDAY & COMPANY, INC., GARDEN CITY, NEW YORK

School is out. School is out! As the bell rang and clattered through the hall the first and second grades spilled out into the October sunshine. School is out. School is out! Red sweaters, plaid skirts, and bright checked dresses made a whirly, twirly pattern across the schoolyard.

"Children. Children!" Miss Parker called from the schoolhouse steps, and for a moment the reds and greens and soft dungaree blues were still. "Don't forget tomorrow is Halloween. Be sure and wear your costumes to school."

"We will!"

"We won't forget!"

"See you tomorrow, Miss Parker."

The children moved on again toward the swings, toward the slides, toward the busses. A few who lived nearby began to walk and hop and skip toward home.

Across the playground the sun sparkled brightly on Danny's glasses as he turned to wave good-by. "I won't forget," Danny called back, and his voice was high and clear and happy. "I won't forget, Miss Parker." Then he started off again toward the little old back road that led down into the valley where he lived.

This morning Danny's mother had said for the first time he could walk home by himself. He didn't even have to wait for Tad and Mike, his twin big brothers in the eighth grade. So now Danny laughed out loud as he skipped along. There was no chance of his forgetting tomorrow. Tomorrow was Halloween AND Danny's birthday. It was his seventh birthday, and he knew it was going to be super-special!

There was going to be a supper party at Uncle Bill's and Aunt Bessie's house. Then there was the surprise combination birthday present that Uncle Bill and Aunt Bessie and Mother and Father were giving him.

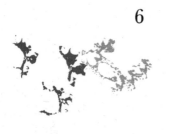

Danny scuffed up an extra-big pile of clean, dry leaves and plopped

down on top of them. The leaves were warm from the sun. They smelled good, and they felt good, and they sounded just wonderful. Danny scooped up great rustling armfuls and made himself a fallen-leaf fort from which he could look down into the valley.

He saw his family's house and right across the cornfield he saw Uncle Bill's and Aunt Bessie's house and the cluster of farm buildings. The corn shocks looked like Indian tepees. For a second Danny thought maybe his surprise combination present was going to be a tent. Then he knew that wasn't right because Aunt Bessie had given him a hint, and the hint was that the name of his present began with B.

Bat, ball, box, bank. Danny thought of all the words he knew that began with B. None of them sounded just right for a surprise combination birthday present. Beaver, bird, bunny. Danny liked animals better than anything in the world. Somehow he did not think his present was going to be a bird or a beaver or a bunny.

His eyes moved on along the valley to Aunt Bessie's vegetable garden. There he saw Barnacle Bland, the scarecrow. B! B! Barnacle Bland was dressed in a sailor suit and a high top hat. He was the finest scarecrow in all the world, and both of his names began with B. But of course Danny knew that Barnacle Bland was not going to be his surprise combination birthday present.

Just then Uncle Bill's farm truck rumbled and rattled across the cornfield. The truck was piled high with corn, and right on top of all the sliding, shining, golden ears was something black. Danny stared and stared at that black thing, and for a minute he even forgot about his birthday. Uncle Bill stopped the truck by the corncrib and got out. Then he reached up and lifted down the black thing. It stretched itself and walked over to the old stone hitching post and clambered up on top of it. Danny laughed out loud.

The black thing was only Inky, Uncle Bill's cat! Inky was so old and stiff that whenever she climbed up on the hitching post she had to meouw and meouw for Uncle Bill or Aunt Bessie when she wanted to come down.

Right now Inky curled herself up for a sun bath on the hitching post and Uncle Bill unloaded his corn. When he was finished he went to the cab of the truck and took out two, four, six, SEVEN big orange pumpkins! Then he put them in a line on the stone wall by the barnyard. When Danny saw them he grinned like a jack-o'-lantern himself. Uncle Bill made the best pumpkin faces and Aunt Bessie made the best pumpkin pie in the whole world, but that wasn't all. Now that Danny saw those seven big, round pumpkins he remembered another hint about his surprise combination birthday present.

You had to be seven, not three or five or even six, but seven years old to own it!

Aunt Bessie and Uncle Bill had come over after supper last Monday to talk to Mother and Father about Danny's birthday. Danny knew it was about that, because before they left Aunt Bessie came up to kiss him good night and told him so.

13

"It's all settled and it begins with a B," she said, and then she had given him the other hint. "We've all just agreed that seven years old is plenty big enough and grown up enough for our surprise combination birthday present."

"Tell me more!" Danny said. He hugged her so close that he could smell the perfume of wild grapes and spices that were still in her hair from jelly making. "Tell me more or I'll bust."

Aunt Bessie had just laughed in the darkness. She laughed the slow, low, pigeon-cote rumble of a laugh that always made Danny feel cozy. But she wouldn't tell him anything more. She wouldn't say a word except that his surprise combination birthday present began with a B. AND that when he was seven he would be big enough and grown up enough to own it.

Right now Danny jumped out of his leaf fort and started down the hill. He took great long striding steps and he felt big enough for anything. For a boat, for a bear, for a big brass band.

Danny reached the bottom of the hill when Mike and Tad flashed past him on their bicycles. "Hi, slow poke!" Mike said, waving a free hand. "Is this as far as you've gone?"

"Hi," Tad said, and for a moment he stood up with both feet in the saddle. "If you'd just learn to bike well you could zoom home."

Then the two big boys put both hands on their handle bars and both feet on their pedals and raced each other along the flat stretch of the lane toward home. Danny stood still and stared after them. His heart sank as though someone had pushed it down like a bicycle pedal. Finally he began

16

to walk again, only now he took slow, sad, heavy steps. Even a little horned snail on the stone wall beside him moved faster than he did.

Danny walked so slowly that he stopped. He stopped because as the big boys biked out of sight he was sure his surprise combination birthday present was going to be a bicycle. Why, 'way back before school last August, Father had even taken him down to the store to look at a bicycle. Father and the big boys had gone all over it and said what a fine bike it was. Then

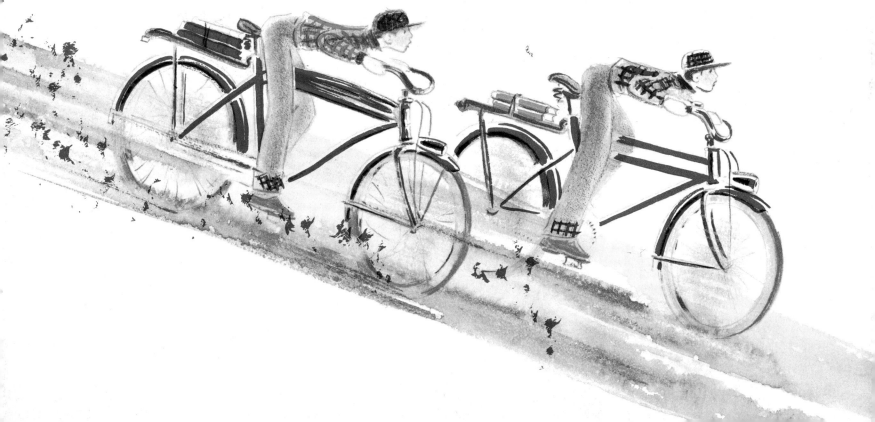

when they went home Danny had had a lesson in bicycle riding, and how he had hated it. Mother and Father, the two big boys, and five-year-old Sally, who was the baby of the family, had all stood and watched while Danny tried riding Mike's bicycle.

Danny had fallen twice, and as soon as the big boys knew he wasn't hurt they had roared with laughter. Then Mother and Father had lifted Sally onto Tad's bike. Sally was so small that her feet hardly touched the pedals, but she was much quicker at learning than Danny.

Well, finally Danny had learned, sort of. But even when he could get off without falling and get on with only one person helping, he didn't like it. Bicycling was either a hot sticky push uphill or a cold scary rush downhill, Danny thought. And he knew he did not want a bicycle of his own for his surprise combination birthday present.

19

Danny began to walk again. Now he didn't hear the rustle of the leaves or smell the peppery autumn smell of bayberries by the old stone wall. He just walked along slowly with his head down. He didn't even look up when Old Siwash, Uncle Bill's mule, put his long neck over the wall, hoping for sugar, or a carrot.

"Danny. Danny. Aren't you coming to see us?" When Danny heard

20

that he turned. There was Aunt Bessie standing beside the stone hitching post stroking Inky.

So Danny went over and Aunt Bessie lifted Inky down and they all went into the kitchen together. Aunt Bessie gave Inky a bowl of milk. Then she gave Danny a glass of milk and three of the chewy brown butternut cookies she had just taken out of the oven. When Danny was finished she let him mix a pailful of corn meal and skim milk for the piglets. Usually Danny liked mixing big beautifully sloshy pailfuls of pig food better than anything. But today he was thinking so hard about his surprise combination present he didn't really enjoy it.

Even when he and Aunt Bessie carried the pail out to the pig pen his mind stayed on bicycles. The five little pigs came running, grunting and squealing for their food. Bratso and Fatso, the biggest piglets came first. Then Waltz and Schmaltz, the next biggest and finally Half Pint, the runt. Half Pint tried so hard to get his share that he put his front feet in the trough. But Danny didn't say a word.

"What's the matter, Danny?" Aunt Bessie said finally. "Did something go wrong at school?"

"School?" Danny said, and the morning seemed as long ago as Christmas. "School? No, I was just wondering — —"

"About your birthday present?" Aunt Bessie asked. Danny looked away from her, and she beamed down at him, pleased with herself for guessing. "I know just how you feel. I remember just before my tenth birthday. I knew my family were going to give me a bicycle and I thought I couldn't stand waiting. But the day finally came, and the bike seemed better than ever because I'd waited for so long."

"Yes," Danny said, and suddenly his throat felt as dry as though he'd swallowed a pine cone. "Well, thanks for the cookies, and now I guess I'd better go home."

He walked the short way down the lane very, very slowly, and now he was more certain than ever that his surprise combination present was going to be a bicycle.

Danny's family were already at supper by the time he reached home. Danny washed his hands and brushed his hair. When he pulled out his chair he saw that Father had his big gold watch on the table in front of him. "You're late," Father said, and snapped the watch back into his pocket. "Half an hour late."

"'Scuse me," Danny said, and began to eat his stew. "I stopped in at Aunt Bessie's and helped her feed the piglets."

"Did you feed your own ducks?" Father asked. "Have they been fed since morning?"

"N-no," Danny said, and felt as though he'd swallowed two pine cones. "No. But I'll feed them after supper."

It was late and dark by the time they had all finished supper. From the kitchen window Danny couldn't even see the barn where the ducks lived. He put bread scraps and carrots into his special basket and pulled

on his sweater. Then as he started out into the darkness he decided he
would like some company.

"Sally," he called back. "Sally, would you like to go with me? You
know you love to feed the ducks."

But Sally was already in her pajamas, brushing her teeth for bed.

"How about one of you?" Danny said to his two big brothers.

"Can't," Mike said, and started up the stairs two steps at a time.
"Homework."

"Can't," Tad said, and headed for the cellar. "I have to finish the jack-o'-lantern I'm making for the school party."

"I'll go," said Mother, "as soon as I've finished the dishes."

"I'll help," said Danny and soon they were on their way. Danny carried Mother's big red flashlight. The light made the barn seem even nicer than it was in the daytime. Danny was in no hurry to leave."

"The ducks are neat," he said as they watched the white one settle down in her straw bed for the night. "If I had three more I'd be able to start a duck farm."

Just then Father came out of the dark, unused side of the barn. "Plenty of room," Father said to Mother, but Danny was so busy watching the two gray ducks that he didn't hear him or see him.

"It's going to be clear and cold tomorrow." Father spoke louder, and this time Danny heard him and jumped like a startled chipmunk. "It'll be a perfect day for Halloween."

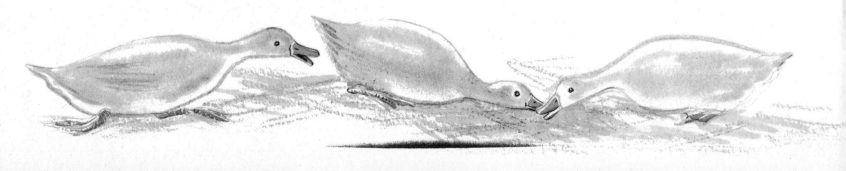

They all walked down to the house together. Then when Danny started upstairs to bed Mother and Father sat down in front of the living-room fire.

"Danny does love animals," Mother said. Danny knew he ought not to be listening, but somehow his feet didn't move along the upstairs hall.

"That's – true – enough!" Father said. Danny could tell from the sound of his voice that he was lighting his pipe as he spoke. "I almost wish we'd bought him rabbits or guinea pigs for his birthday. Still, you and Bessie were both sure seven was grown up enough for . . ."

Danny never heard for what. Just then Mike and Tad clattered through the hall and he had to go on to his own little bedroom. He undressed quickly and turned off the light. As he put his toes down between the clean, icy sheets he was sure, cold-clammy sure, about the bicycle.

The next morning when Danny woke up he could see that Father had been right about the weather. It was so cold that the fields were still quilted with frost and so clear that Danny could see a thin blue curl of wood smoke going up from Uncle Bill's chimney.

Danny put his Indian suit over his school clothes and dashed downstairs for breakfast. Mother must have cooked something extra-special because the house smelled sweet and spicy and just right for Halloween.

"Many happy returns, Danny boy," Mother said. "And Happy Halloween. I hope you have a lovely day and that you like being seven."

"Thanks," Danny said, "and Miss Parker told us to wear our costumes to school, so can I keep on my Indian suit?"

"Of course," Mother said. "But now eat your breakfast."

So Danny ate country sausage and spiced apple fritters. As he ate he felt much more cheerful than he had last night. Perhaps he had guessed wrong about getting a bicycle. Or perhaps if he had guessed right the grown-ups would let him sell it. Then he could buy chickens or guinea pigs or loads more ducks.

It was a good day at school and a good day at home. By half-past four Danny knew he liked being seven. He had walked home quickly and without stopping. He had fed his ducks without being reminded. He had remembered to bring home the pumpkin card he had made at school for Mother and Father at the Halloween party. And he still had enough time left so that he could make another card to take to Uncle Bill and Aunt Bessie.

Danny had just started drawing when Sally bounced into his room in the rabbit suit that the big boys and Danny himself had worn when they

were little. "Look at me!" Sally said.
"I can hop like a rabbit."

"Neat," Danny said, and began coloring. "Fine!"

"Danny, darling, are you coming?" Mother put her head around the door just as Danny drew in some fine jagged pumpkin teeth. "I promised Aunt Bessie that Sally and I'd drive over early so that I could help with supper. Father's going straight from work, and the big boys are going to bicycle."

"I'll walk," Danny said, because he seemed to walk faster now he was seven. "It won't take me two minutes."

So Mother and Sally drove off and Danny went on with his drawing. For a few minutes there wasn't any sound in the house except the tick of the big hall clock. Then as Mike and Tad began to dress for the party the house rang with bumps and scuffles and laughs and giggles.

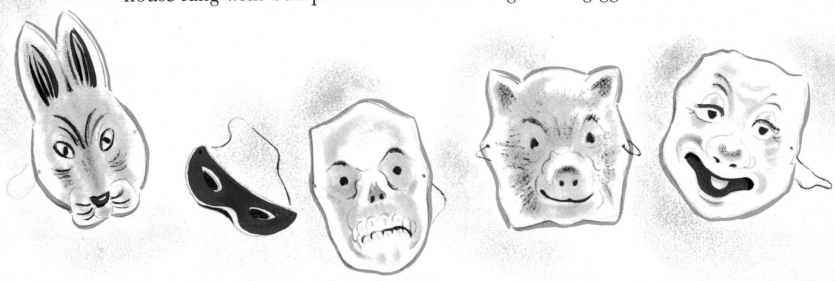

Last week Mother had taken all four children down to the store to choose Halloween masks. Tad had picked out a devil mask. Mike had chosen a rhino's face with one yellow tusk. Neither of the big boys would tell a soul what he was going to be at the Halloween-birthday party. Even now Danny couldn't tell from the sounds whether they were going to be scary or funny.

Just then the front door slammed. The next instant the house was tick-tock quiet again. So Danny knew he wouldn't find out until he went to the party. He finished his pumpkin card and put on the ghost mask he had chosen. The ghost mask looked fine above the Indian suit, but when Danny tried to put on his feather headdress above that it didn't fit.

For a minute Danny didn't know what to do, and then he had a really good idea. He had two long turkey feathers that Aunt Bessie had given him. If he could just fasten those to his head with string they'd be better than his headdress. He looked in his treasure chest and he looked in back of the bookcase. He looked in Sally's room and he looked in the kitchen. Then he remembered that he had seen the turkey feathers in the croquet box on the front porch.

The feathers were still there. When Danny tied them on to the back of his head he looked like a very ghostly Indian.

He left the house and hurried along the lane toward Uncle Bill's and Aunt Bessie's. He could just see the seven jack-o'-lanterns lighting the way to the back door before he remembered his cards. He turned right around and ran back home to get them. He was sure – well, almost sure – he'd left the cards on his bureau. They weren't there and he finally found them under his schoolbooks, which was where he had put them in the first place.

He started off again and now it was very dark out and much colder. Danny shivered inside his Indian suit and scuttled along the side of the lane as fast as he could go. The leaves rustled at his feet, but somehow it wasn't the same cheerful sound that it was in the daylight. There were other noises too. There were creakings and snappings behind the stone wall. And overhead there was the cold, lonely wail of the wind blowing through the telephone wires.

Danny pushed his cards into his pockets and ran until he had to stop for breath. He had reached Uncle Bill's lawn by that time. He walked more and more slowly while his heart thumped faster and faster. Danny wasn't scared, of course. It was just that the bushes looked so big and black in the darkness. If the twins had put on scary costumes and were going to jump out at him this was where they would do it.

The farmhouse curtains were drawn and there was no light except from the jack-o'-lantern. The jack-o'-lanterns were set out wide apart from each other. Danny knew from last year that they made a path around the house to the back door.

He went so close to the first jack-o'-lantern that he could see the pumpkin seeds Uncle Bill had used for teeth. He touched the cold round shell of the pumpkin for luck. Then he hurried through the deep, black shadows to the next one. He stood still for a second as though he were playing Red Light-Green Light. Then he scurried on to the third pumpkin.

By the time Danny reached the sixth pumpkin he was in the pitch-blackness between the barn and the woodshed. He could see the seventh and biggest jack-o'-lantern quite a long way ahead of him. He guessed it was on top of the old stone hitching post by the kitchen door and took one step toward it. He took two steps, and then a queer thing happened!

One minute that big bright grin was straight ahead of him. Then there was a thud and the grin flickered out into darkness.

Danny took two steps backward, and his heart thumped faster than ever. He stared over to where the grin had been and then he saw the eyes. They were cold, round greeny eyes. They stared down at him from where the jack-o'-lantern had been only a second before.

For an instant Danny was scared. So scared that his breath stopped and his hair prickled up under his Indian feathers. Then there was a loud angry "Meouw" and Danny started to breathe again. It was only Inky! Inky had knocked over the pumpkin face when she'd clambered up onto her favorite seat on top of the hitching post.

"Here, Inky, here, Puss!" Danny said. Just then the barn door behind him began to open.

Danny didn't hear the door or see the door, but by the thin sliver of light that came through it he saw more of Inky. Inky's back was arched. She was frightened and angry and spitting. Danny stared. Then he saw why Inky was frightened! He saw teeth and a long gray face just below Inky. The body, if there was one, was still lost in shadows.

When Danny saw that face his skin crawled. He didn't know whether it was a spook, or a wild beast, or a big boy playing tricks. He didn't care, either. No matter what it was, Danny knew he didn't like it. He wanted to run into Uncle Bill's house or hide his eyes and yell for Mother. Then as Inky meowed again he knew he couldn't! Inky's leg was so stiff that she couldn't get off the hitching post unless someone helped her.

Danny gave an Indian warwhoop to make himself feel braver. Then he rushed toward the hitching post. At the same time the kitchen door in front of him opened wide. In that sudden burst of light Danny saw everything. He saw the gray face had long, long ears and that now the teeth were covered by soft furry lips. It wasn't a spook, or a wild beast, or a mean boy trying to scare Inky. It was a small gray donkey!

Aunt Bessie and Uncle Bill, Mother and Sally and Father were all out of the kitchen door by that time, and someone shouted, "Happy Birthday, Danny! The burro is your surprise combination birthday present beginning with B!"

Aunt Bessie lifted Inky down from the hitching post, and Inky rushed off toward the barn just as Tad and Mike came out of it. Tad was dressed in Barnacle Bland's clothes and the devil mask. Mike was dressed in an old worn-out evening dress with the rhino's face on top of that.

"Boys!" Father said. "You promised me there wouldn't be any scaring —"

43

"There wasn't. By us, anyway," Tad said, and then Father lifted Danny onto the donkey's warm furry back.

Danny touched the neat black cross on the donkey's shoulders. He patted his neck and picked up the reins that Father gave him. Uncle Bill turned on the yard light, and Danny rode the little donkey three times all the way around the barnyard.

"The burro's name is Lucky," Aunt Bessie said when Danny stopped to give Sally a ride. "Do you really like him?"

"L-like him!" Danny said, and he was so excited and happy his words were shaky.

Just then Lucky reached out and nibbled at the edge of the Halloween cards that were still in Danny's pocket. Danny gave the cards away. He found a little corn candy in the bottom of his pocket and gave that to Lucky. The donkey ate it all up and nudged Danny's shoulder for more.

Everybody laughed when they saw that, and Aunt Bessie said: "Then everyone's pleased except Inky. She will be when you take Lucky back to live in your own barn. Inky was jealous when we tied Lucky to her hitching post."

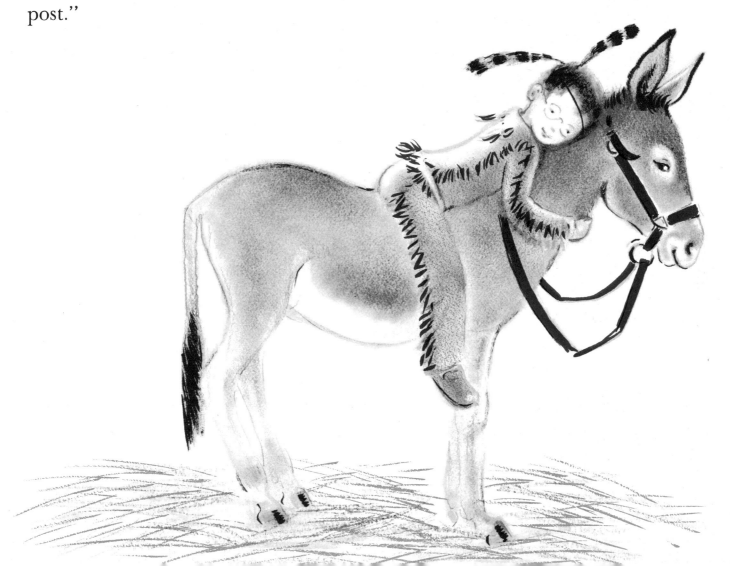

When Danny heard that, he told them how he'd first seen the lighted pumpkin and then Inky's eyes and Lucky's teeth. He told them just how scared he'd been when he knew he'd have to rescue Inky.

"Supper's ready!" Aunt Bessie said when Danny had finished his story. "Who is hungry enough to eat birthday cake and pumpkin pie for dessert?"

"I am," Tad said.

"I am," Mike said

"Me too," said Sally, and they all trooped into the farmhouse.

Danny stayed behind long enough to make sure that Lucky was warm and cozy in one of Uncle Bill's empty stalls. When he finally turned away he saw that Father was waiting for him just outside the barn door.

"Now I know you're big enough!" Father said. He swung Danny up on his shoulders so that he was higher than the corncrib. "A boy that's ready to rescue a lame cat on Halloween is grown up enough and brave enough for a combination birthday present of a burro!"

Date Due